Distributed by Childrens Press,
Chicago, Illinois 60656

Library of Congress Cataloging in Publication Data

Moncure, Jane Belk.
  Play with i and g / by Jane Belk Moncure ; illustrated by Jodie
McCallum.
    p. cm. — (Alphabet books)
  Summary: A brief tale emphasizing the uses of "i" and "g" in
various words.
  ISBN 0-89565-507-1
  [1. Alphabet.]   I. McCallum, Jodie, ill.   II. Title.
III. Series.
PZ7.M739Pi   1989
[E]—dc20   89-17271
                                             CIP
                                             AC

1 2 3 4 5 6 7 8 9 10 11 12 R 97 96 95 94 93 92 91 90 89

Play With and

by Jane Belk Moncure
illustrated by Jodie McCallum

THE CHILD'S WORLD

ELGIN, ILLINOIS 60121

Starring the letters

i and g

The publisher wishes to thank the letters "i" and "g." Without them, this book would not be possible.

This is little

This is little g

and play.

What can we be?

This is little P

May I play?

What can we three be?

Pig.
Play pig.

Do what pig can do.

This is little W

May I play?

What can we three be?

Wig.

Play with a wig!

What is that?

A wig on a pig!

A piggy-wiggy.

A wiggy-piggy.

This is little j

May I play?

What can we three be?

Jig.

Dance a jig!

Dance a jig, pig.

Dance a
jig . . .

pig in a wig!

What is that?

A pig . . . on a wig.

Off the wig, pig.

Good-by, wig.

Good-by, pig.

Good-by, jig.

i and g

also play with

b and d

Can you?